Silent Screams

Helen Sawyer

Published by Helen Sawyer, 2024.

This is a work of fiction. Similarities to real people, places, or events are entirely coincidental.

SILENT SCREAMS

First edition. July 30, 2024.

Copyright © 2024 Helen Sawyer.

ISBN: 979-8227134219

Written by Helen Sawyer.

Also by Helen Sawyer

Silent Screams

SILENT SCREAMS

A Chilling Novel

by

Helen Sawyer

Preface

For as long as I can remember, I have been captivated by the supernatural—the unknown that lurks in the shadows, the whispers in the dark, and the stories that send shivers down our spines. This fascination has been the driving force behind my writing career, leading me to explore haunted houses, ancient curses, and the chilling tales that live on in our collective imagination. "Silent Screams" is the culmination of years of curiosity, research, and an unyielding desire to uncover the truth behind the most enigmatic and terrifying legends.

The journey to write "Silent Screams" began on a cold, autumn afternoon while I was visiting a quaint town nestled in the heart of New England. I was there on a research trip, hoping to gather material for my next book, when I stumbled upon Whispering Lane. The locals spoke of it in hushed tones, their faces a mix of fear and reverence whenever the old Hartwell mansion was mentioned. It seemed like the name carried history and sorrow they couldn't escape.

My interest was piqued. I had to know more. The Hartwell family's story, their rise to prominence, and the tragic events that unfolded within their grand estate became an obsession. The more I dug into the town's archives, the more I realized that this was no ordinary haunted house. It was a place steeped in a complex web of love, loss, and a descent into madness.

As an author, I've always believed in the power of first-hand experience. So, with a mix of excitement and trepidation, I decided to spend time at the Hartwell mansion. I wanted to walk its halls, feel its oppressive atmosphere, and perhaps, if I was fortunate or unfortunate enough, catch a glimpse of the spirits that were said to haunt its rooms.

During my stay, I meticulously documented my experiences and the stories I uncovered. I spent countless hours in the mansion's library, sifting through old letters, journals, and photographs, piecing together the narrative of the Hartwell family. Each discovery was like finding a piece of a dark, intricate puzzle. The attic, the forbidden rituals, the tragic death of Emily Hartwell, and Thomas Hartwell's desperate, terrifying attempts to bridge the gap between the living and the dead—all of these elements coalesced into a story that needed to be told.

Writing "Silent Screams" was a deeply personal journey. It forced me to confront my own fears and question the nature of obsession and loss. The Hartwell mansion, with its dark history and haunting presence, became a character in its own right, guiding me through the narrative with its silent screams.

Through Helen Donovan, my protagonist, I found a voice that resonated with my own—an unrelenting seeker of truth, driven by an insatiable curiosity and a desire to bring light to the darkest corners of history. Her journey through Whispering Lane mirrors my own exploration, as both of us grappled with the shadows of the past and the lingering echoes of sorrow.

"Silent Screams" is more than a ghost story—it's a testament to love's endurance and our willingness to hold onto it despite unimaginable horror. It is a reminder that some secrets, no matter how deeply buried, will always find a way to the surface, demanding to be heard.

I invite you, dear reader, to join Helen Donovan on her journey through the haunted halls of the Hartwell mansion. As you turn the pages, you may feel the chill of the unknown, the suspense of the unraveling mystery, and the silent screams that echo through time.

Thank you for embarking on this journey with me.

Sincerely,

Helen Sawyer

Prologue

The Whispering Lane mansion stood outside the town like a sentinel from bygone eras. After years of disrepair, the once-domestic and majestic Victorian edifice seemed to be sagging. As it climbed up its brick exterior, ivy spread, and the dusty, gloomy windows looked outward like the empty eyes of a giant long since dead. The villagers steered clear of it, deterred by their hushed stories of curses and spirits. But even in its run-down condition, there was something irresistible about the house—a call that resonated with those who could hear the ghosts of the past.

One such soul was Helen Donovan, who was attracted to the secrets that lurked beyond the ancient mansion's walls for unknown reasons. She was a writer by trade and had always been enthralled with paranormal tales. Her writing career was based on solving the mysteries of haunted homes and paranormal activity, which she then turned into best-selling books that enthralled her readers. However, the residence on Whispering Lane was distinct. It was more than simply a narrative; it was a riddle that cried out to be answered and a past that awaited discovery.

Helen had arrived on the farm on a cold autumn day. The promise of rain and the smell of rotting leaves were carried by the wind as it rustled through the trees. She felt a wave of anxiety and eagerness build as she got closer to the front door. In her palm, the key she had taken from the town's historical society felt weighty and frigid. After a little pause, she put it into the lock and twisted.

The entryway was musty and gloomy, and the door creaked open. As they drifted through the air, dust particles caught the light from the open doorway. Helen entered, her footsteps resonating across the deserted hallway. With the weight of untold tales, the quiet in the home hummed with life. Shutting the door behind her, she disconnected from the outer world and totally embraced the ambiance of the ancient home.

As she investigates the home, Helen's thoughts begin to intertwine with the narrative. Constructed in the late 1800s, the mansion was a symbol of the Hartwell family's riches and social standing. The prosperous businessman Thomas Hartwell had moved in with his wife Elizabeth and their two kids, Emily and Jacob. That bliss, however, did not last long for the family. Emily's illness and death were tragic events, and Thomas, unable to deal with the loss, turned to the occult in a last-ditch effort to bring her back. His fixation had driven him insane, and the once-happy house had turned into a haven of terror and hopelessness.

Though Helen's investigation had yielded the essential details, she was certain that there was more to the tale. She was desperate to learn the truth, since the murmurs from the townsfolk suggested sinister rituals and restless ghosts. Her flashlight created unsettling shadows on the fading pictures and peeling wallpaper as she made her way around the rooms. Though the attic beckoned to her the most, every chamber had its own mysteries.

The door to the attic was locked, as she had been informed. Her key did not fit when she tried it. She made a mental note to come back with tools to pick the lock, frustrated but unfazed. For the time being, she focused on exploring the remainder of the home in hopes of discovering hints that would lead her to the solutions she was looking for.

Her next destination was the library, a space with shelves crammed with antiquated records and volumes. Here, she discovered a bundle of letters bound with a frayed ribbon, which turned out to be the first genuine piece of the puzzle. Elizabeth Hartwell wrote the letters to her sister, Margaret. Helen started to see a picture of a family ripped apart by fear and sadness as she went through it.

Elizabeth wrote in her letters about the unusual happenings that had started to afflict the home, as well as Thomas's growing preoccupation with the occult. She described shadows moving on their own, whispering in the night, and a pervasive feeling of dread around every turn. Elizabeth had made an effort to keep her kids safe, but Thomas's insanity had overcome him, resulting in a disastrous showdown that destroyed the family.

Helen's heart hurt for Elizabeth; she was the victim of a nightmare from which she was unable to awaken. The sudden conclusion of the letters left Helen with more questions than answers. What had transpired throughout the last several days? What had Thomas let loose in his desperate attempt to reunite with Emily? More importantly, how could Helen calm the agitated spirits?

Helen kept exploring, her head buzzing with possibilities, determined to find out. She was ready to confront whatever darkness lied behind the walls of the mansion because she knew it contained the answers she needed. Helen shivered as the sun descended outside, casting long shadows over the floorboards. At dusk, the mansion appeared to come to life, its secrets whispering just out of reach.

The opening of "Silent Screams" sets the tone for an expedition into uncharted territory in an attempt to learn the truth about the terrible history of the Hartwell family. It's a story about obsession, loss, and the lingering presence of the paranormal. Helen will learn that some secrets are best kept hidden and that the past may still call out to those who are brave enough to look for it as she explores the mystery surrounding the home on Whispering Lane.

Chapter 1

The House on Whispering Lane

The crumbling Victorian home at the end of Whispering Lane loomed menacingly behind the dusk curtain. Ivy clambered up the walls like skeletal fingers, holding on to the shattered windows that stared forth like hollow eyes. Even though it was a beautiful summer evening, there seemed to be a palpable chill in the air around it. For as long as anybody could remember, the house had been the subject of a long-running local legend, whispering secrets of the past like a dark shadow against the horizon.

Helen had been told stories of the haunted mansion, strange activities, and ghostly presences. Her pals would talk about it all the time, lowering their voices to whispers whenever they brought up the ancient mansion. Some reported seeing shadows moving and people in the windows when nobody should have been there. Others noticed strange sounds coming from within the walls, like whispers carried by the wind. However, Helen was a cynic who consistently discounted these tales as the product of hyperactive minds.

But tonight, she was standing in front of the notorious house's wrought-iron gates. Being a writer, she was always searching for new ideas, and the mystery surrounding the home on Whispering Lane had captured her interest. Maybe it was the difficulty of dispelling the myths, or maybe there was a more profound, mysterious need to face uncertainty. For whatever reason, she was driven to learn the truth about the house's troubled history.

As she opened the gate, it made a creaking sound that reverberated through the night's silence. Her feet were unsteady because of the uneven cobblestones and overgrown weeds on the walk leading to the front door. She couldn't get rid of the sense that someone was watching her as she got closer to the home. Because the feeling was so intense, she kept peeking over her shoulder, almost expecting to see someone or something hiding in the shadows.

The front porch sagged under her weight, and the wood creaked menacingly. The house sounded as if it were annoyed by her presence. She hesitated as she stood in front of the door, her fingers lingering over the chilly brass knocker. She felt a shudder go down her spine as a burst of wind rustled the leaves. She thought for a second about going back, but her curiosity overruled her. Three knocks later, the sound still echoes in the still night.

With a slow, unsettling groan, the door swung wide to reveal a dimly illuminated corridor. With her heart racing in her chest, Helen entered. It was a summer evening, and the air inside the house was considerably cooler than it should have been. She looked around, taking in the sight of the opulent staircase, the dust-covered chandelier, and the peeling, faded wallpaper on the walls. There was a sense of neglect—something lost and abandoned about the home.

She heard the smallest murmur, like a breath on her ear, as she moved further into the corridor. She strained to listen as she froze, but the sound vanished as soon as it appeared. She brushed it off with her imagination and continued on her journey. She went inside a sitting room first, which had worn-out furniture wrapped in white linens. The ceiling had cobwebs hanging from its corners, and the fireplace was chilly and gloomy. She had a peculiar feeling of familiarity despite the chaos, as if she had visited this place before in a previous life.

She proceeded to the dining area, where a long table was positioned under an old, dusty chandelier. There were shattered dishes and tarnished silverware on the table, as if it had been prepared for a dinner that had never been served. It seemed as if everyone had hurried out, packing up all they had. Helen wondered what happened to them and why they left this beautiful old home.

The room was filled with an unsettling, disembodied hum as the whispers started up again, louder this time. Helen felt her heartbeat increase, and she pivoted to find the cause. Even though no one was there, there was a palpable sense of being watched. With a worried look in her eyes, she retreated from the dining area.

Driven by an unexplained need, she decided to go upstairs. The massive, opulent staircase made a creaking sound as she walked on its wooden steps. The murmurs became louder and more forceful as she climbed higher. They surrounded her, seeming to approach from all directions, and she began to feel fearful. After climbing the stairs, she emerged onto a long, narrow corridor that had many locked doors.

She tried two doors: one that led to a tiny, unoccupied bedroom, and the other that was locked. The third door caused her to halt. As she went for the handle, the murmurs intensified into a cacophony, as if to warn her to keep away. Her palm trembled as she hesitated, but her curiosity overcame her. She pushed the door open after turning the doorknob.

The little, dirty window's single source of light was dim, and the room was black. Her eyes adjusting to the darkness, she noticed that it was a child's bedroom, complete with toys strewn over the floor and a little bed covered in a tattered quilt. This chamber seemed different from the others, and it sent a shiver down her spine. It seemed alive, like it held a previous inhabitants' spirit.

As she entered, the door behind her banged. Helen felt her heart spring into her throat. She whirled around, attempting to unlock it, but it was securely closed. The voices became louder and more desperate, and panic struck. Removing herself from the doorway, she surveyed the space, searching for any indication of the source of the disturbance.

She suddenly became aware of the little wooden rocking horse in the corner. With a startling creak, it started to move, first slowly and then more quickly, swaying back and forth. When Helen realized she wasn't alone, her breath seized in her throat. A dark silhouette emerged in the room's corner, almost discernible due to the low lighting. It was a youngster—a little girl with sunken eyes and long, black hair.

The girl opened her lips, but nothing came out. Rather, the murmur of whispers appeared to come from every direction around her, taking up the room with their dark murmur. With her thoughts whirling, Helen stepped back. She wanted to cry out and flee, but she was immobile and couldn't take her gaze off the ethereal apparition.

Helen followed the small girl's point to a location on the floor. Under the worn blanket, there was a discreet little space. Mustering up her courage, she bent down and removed the duvet to show a slightly elevated wooden floorboard. She pryed it apart to discover a little, dusty box below.

Her hands shaking, she opened the package. Inside, there were letters, old photos, and a journal. As she turned through the pages of the journal, she began to piece together the history of the home on Whispering Lane. The journal belonged to Emily, a little child who had spent many years living in the home with her family. Emily wrote of weird experiences, including dark figures she saw and words she heard throughout the night. She wrote about her anxiety and the way a malicious spirit appeared to come alive in the house.

The last entry was the most terrifying. Emily described in her writings how she had uncovered a sinister secret—something that had cursed the home and all of its occupants. She pleaded with whoever discovered the journal to find the truth and liberate the spirits. Sara felt terrible for the girl and her fear. She came to understand that Emily's ghost was still imprisoned in the mansion and would not be freed until the truth was discovered.

Helen studied the letters and photos again, determined to assist, piece by piece, with the jigsaw being put together. She learned that Emily's father had been experimenting with superhuman abilities via dark and occult activities. Something wicked that had cursed the home and condemned its occupants had been released by his acts. The voices in the whispers belonged to those who had endured suffering and were stuck in a never-ending circle of agony.

Helen was aware of her obligations. To drive out evil and free the imprisoned spirits, she had to carry out a purification rite. She picked up the necessities from around the house: sage, salt, and a white candle. The whispers became more urgent and louder as she got ready for the ceremony. She realized there was not much time left, so she felt compelled to act.

She began the ceremony by lighting the candle and sage and reciting the words she had discovered in Emily's journal. The tension in the room increased, and the shadows seemed to come to life, writhing and twisting. But Helen didn't back down; her voice remained firm and powerful. The whispering immediately ceased as she finished the ceremony, and the room was flooded with dazzling brightness.

As the light went off, Helen found herself standing by herself in the now-quiet room. In place of the suffocating environment, there was a sense of tranquility. She was aware that Emily and the others could now finally rest in peace and that the spirits had been set free. She went back downstairs, feeling satisfied and accomplished despite her exhaustion.

As she went outdoors, the first morning rays were peeking over the horizon. With its troubled history finally put to rest, the home on Whispering Lane lay still and quiet. Helen was certain that the tale she had discovered would enthrall her audience and be worthy of being told. More significantly, however, she had contributed to the long-lasting resolution of the uneasy ghosts that had plagued the home.

She gave herself one more look before turning to go. The home no longer had the old shadows cast by its windows, like if it were watching her. She grinned, finally feeling satisfied. Both she and the house on Whispering Lane had at last found peace.

Chapter 2

Echoes of the Past

The home on Whispering Lane was at last at peace, even if Helen could not hear the noises of the past. After the terrible events of the previous night, she found herself with more questions than answers. Determined to find out the full truth, she made the decision to research the history of the home. Armed with Emily's notebook and a newfound sense of purpose, she went to the library in the next town to see if any further clues could be found on the house and its former occupants.

Helen entered the library, her senses overwhelmed by the aroma of worn volumes and polished wood. She went up to the front desk, where Mrs. Whitaker, the kind elderly librarian, was going through a stack of books.

Helen said, her desire evident in her voice, "Pardon me, Mrs. Whitaker." I want to know more about the ancient Victorian home at Whispering Lane's end. Are there any archives or records you can share?

At the name of the home, Mrs. Whitaker's eyes widened slightly, and she glanced up. With a hint of interest and caution, she replied, "Ah, the infamous Whispering Lane house." It's been the focus of several regional folktales. I think the archive room has some historical documents and old newspapers. Listen to me.

Helen trailed after Mrs. Whitaker into the dimly lit archive room, which was stacked with tall shelves holding ancient newspapers and documents. The librarian gestured to a rear-facing area. "Move onto them first. Perhaps you will find something helpful.

Helen poured over the data for hours, running her fingertips over the aged newspaper and document print. She discovered that Thomas and Elizabeth Hartwell, a rich couple who had relocated to the town in search of a new beginning, had constructed the home in the late 1800s. Their wealth and hopes for a prosperous future were represented by the mansion. However, as she continued reading, she learned that the family had experienced a string of terrible incidents.

The first tragedy occurred when Emily, their small daughter, had a serious illness. She died at home because no doctor could help her, even with their money. As Helen read Emily's obituary—the Emily whose diary she now owned—her heart wrenched. The murmurs she had heard were probably Emily's screams for assistance, reverberations of her anguish.

Helen discovered more sinister truths the further she went. Thomas Hartwell had developed an obsession with occultism, thinking he could contact his dead daughter and bring her back to life. A slew of inexplicable deaths and disappearances in the town resulted from his more risky and desperate experiments. Fear developed among the locals, and rumors of sinister rituals and evil spirits started to circulate.

Helen's studies were halted by the sound of footsteps. As she glanced up, she saw a towering, menacing person standing in the doorway. Mr. Granger was a well-known town historian with a wealth of local folklore.

Mr. Granger's powerful voice reverberated through the tiny space as he remarked, "I couldn't help but notice your interest in the Hartwell house." "It's rare that someone visits that location in search of answers."

Helen nodded, her feelings conflicting between relief and caution. "I discovered Emily Hartwell's journal. I think she and other spirits are stuck in the house. How to fix what went wrong and make things right between them.

Mr. Granger's countenance became gentler. "Emily has a heartbreaking tale to tell. Their family was destroyed by her father's occult fixation. Many people think that by performing certain rites, he was able to establish a portal to another planet and let evil spirits into our reality. The home's inhabitants' terror and misery made it a beacon for these things.

Helen shuddered as the realization began to settle on her. "Is there a way to release the spirits and shut that doorway?"

Mr. Granger gave a slow nod. "It's risky, but there are methods. The spirits need to be led back to their domain, and the rituals need to be reversed. You will need Emily's particular talisman, and the ceremony must be carried out in the center of the home, where the portal was first opened.

Helen's thoughts raced as she thought about the possible outcomes. Although Emily's journal had previously been located, she still wanted something more intimate, something that had a deep emotional link to the girl. She said thank you to Mr. Granger and made her way back to the home, determined to locate the talisman and carry out the ceremony.

Helen had a fresh sense of purpose when she got back home. An air of eagerness appeared to permeate the formerly ominous mood. She started looking through Emily's bedroom's artifacts for clues. Under the bed, among the toys and trinkets, she discovered a little locket with an aged appearance. There was a little picture of Emily inside, as well as a strand of her hair. She was aware that this was the talisman she needed.

She had a rush of energy as she grasped the locket, like if Emily were directing her. She headed toward the enormous room in the center of the mansion, where Thomas Hartwell had performed his rites. The dimly lit room's atmosphere was heavy with the weight of many secrets. After setting the locket on the ground, she started getting ready for the ceremony.

Helen surrounded the locket with a ring of white candles, the flickering flames creating unsettling shadows on the walls. She erected a barrier around herself with salt to keep out any ghosts that might attempt to get in the way. She inhaled deeply and started chanting the lines she had discovered in Emily's journal, pleading with the spirits to grant her request.

The temperature dropped, and the shadows seemed to shift on their own. The whispers came again, louder and more forceful, creating a cacophony of voices around the room. Despite her racing heart, Helen kept up the chant, her voice becoming louder with each syllable. The candles flickered erratically, as if mysterious forces would extinguish them.

The chamber was suddenly flooded with a brilliant light as she approached the ritual's peak, and the whispering came to an abrupt end. As the atmosphere became silent, a feeling of calm descended over the house. Helen turned to find Emily's spectral form beside her, her eyes beaming with appreciation.

Emily said, her voice almost audible, "Thank you." "You've released us."

Helen saw Emily's soul fade and disappear into the light. Knowing that she had contributed to providing closure for the restless spirits imprisoned in the mansion, she had a feeling of relief and satisfaction. She was alone in the quiet room when the light went off, and the stifling pressure finally subsided.

Helen meticulously recorded her experiences in the days that followed. Her second book, a suspenseful story about haunted buildings and ghostly remnants of the past, was built on the notes and observations she made. She was certain that the narrative would enthrall her readers, but more than anything, it gave her a feeling of finality.

The Whispering Lane mansion was no longer a source of terror and agony. Now that the spirits were released, it symbolized hope and human resilience. Helen felt grateful and at ease as she made her last visit to the residence. As a reminder of Emily's presence and the love that transcended time and distance, she placed the locket on the mantle.

As she left, the sun was setting, bathing the home in a warm light. The gentle rustling of leaves in the air had replaced the whispering. As a memento of her journey and the individuals she had impacted, Helen knew the home would always have a particular place in her heart.

Chapter 3

The Ghost in the Attic

Helen had finished the ceremony to release the souls who were imprisoned, and the home on Whispering Lane had been quiet for weeks. An unsettling silence has taken the place of the suffocating atmosphere. However, Helen could still feel the effects of her past experiences. She was plagued by the unsettling sensation that something was still unsettled and that there was still something there.

At the base of the grand staircase, Helen stared at the sky. It had just been the attic that she hadn't looked everywhere. Its door had been locked, and she'd failed miserably to get past it. But now that the other spirits were at peace, she was even more determined to find out what was up above.

Every step she took up the stairs seemed to reverberate through the quiet of the home, louder than the one before it. The temperature dropped, and the previously absent uneasiness started to return. When she arrived at the top of the steps, the ancient, splintered wood of the attic door greeted her.

She inhaled deeply before reaching for the doorknob. She was shocked to see it turn readily in her palm. With a squeak, the door opened to expose a tiny, dark stairway that led up to the attic. After a brief pause, she took a flashlight out of her backpack and started to climb.

Huge, dust-caked boxes, trunks, and worn-out furniture were scattered around the vast attic. The smell of decay and long-forgotten recollections pervaded the air. With a quick flick of her flashlight, Helen was able to bring to light the long-forgotten artifacts from the past.

She felt a shiver as she descended deeper into the attic, which had nothing to do with the outside temperature. It was a prickling sensation on the back of her neck, a sense that she was being observed. She pivoted, and the beam flickered over some motion hidden in the darkness.

"Hello?" she said, a little shaky in her voice. "Is anyone there?"

The ancient windows creaked slightly with the little breeze, but there was no reply. She walked a few more steps, her light illuminating the little, dusty rocker in the corner. That's when she heard it—a soft, almost undetectable whisper that sounded like a breath across her ear.

"Helen..."

She froze as her heart thumped in her chest. The tone was kind, even beseeching. With a leisurely turn, she revealed the silhouette of a person standing in the shadows with her flashlight beam. The boy's eyes were wide with fright; he couldn't have been more than eleven.

"Who are you?" Helen inquired, hardly raising her voice beyond a whisper.

With such menacing eyes, the lad just gazed at her without saying anything. She stepped forward, and he was gone, like a wisp of smoke melting into the night. As she stood there, trying to make sense of what she had seen, her mind was racing.

Helen started doing a more comprehensive investigation of the attic, determined to learn the boy's tale. She rummaged through boxes and opened trunks, discovering letters, old clothing, and pictures. She discovered a bundle of papers wrapped with a fading ribbon inside an ancient wooden trunk. One of the items was an old, yellowed diary.

She took a seat on an old crate and started reading, the pages illuminated by the faint glimmer of her flashlight. The diary belonged to a little boy called Jacob, who, in the early 1900s, had resided in the home with his family. As she read, she learned that Emily Hartwell, the girl whose soul she had liberated, had a younger brother named Jacob.

Jacob wrote a lot in his journals about his everyday activities, his love for his family, and his close relationship with his sister. However, the journal's tone got worse as she continued to read. Throughout the night, he described feeling like someone was watching him, seeing dark figures, and hearing whispers. Although his parents wrote off his anxieties as negative dreams, Jacob sensed that something wasn't right.

The most unsettling entries were the last ones. Jacob wrote about Thomas Hartwell, his father, and his spiral into insanity. Thomas had developed an obsession with occultism and thought he could raise Emily from the grave. Jacob told the story of how, with Jacob's consent, his father conducted sinister rites in the attic. The last post described a dreadful night when things went terribly wrong. In his writings, Jacob spoke of a shadowy figure who materialized during the ceremony and carried him off.

Helen's hands were shaking as she closed the diary. Now she knew why Jacob's soul was still imprisoned in the attic and why it had stayed shut. Since he had been a victim of his father's insanity, his soul had never achieved tranquility. She was determined to assist him and understood that, in order to do so, she would have to carry out another ceremony that would set Jacob free and close the door that Thomas Hartwell had opened.

She grabbed everything she needed: salt, candles, and the locket she had previously used. She laid them out in a circle on the attic floor to form a safety barrier. The room felt colder, and the shadows seemed to draw in about her as she lit the candles.

She inhaled deeply and started reciting the sentences she had studied from Emily's journal. Tension filled the air as the shadows twisted and writhed, creating the appearance of a towering, dark person. It was a powerful presence—a dark energy that appeared to drain the room's light itself.

Helen calmly yelled out, "Jacob, I am here to help you," despite the panic that was engulfing her. "I am aware of what happened to you. I'm aware that your father included you in his ceremonies. It's time to move on and let go."

As the dark figure approached, Helen had a sudden and overwhelming feeling of gloom. She chanted on, her will unwavering and her voice becoming more powerful. As the darkness started to fade, she saw the little child, Jacob, standing in the middle of the circle.

Her voice was soothing and kind as she stated, "Jacob, you can be free now." "You don't have to be afraid anymore."

She noticed the dread and agony in the boy's eyes start to diminish as their gaze met hers. Helen remained resolute despite the furious howl from the dark entity behind her. Her hand went out, and Jacob accepted it. His little fingers were thin and icy.

A last, loud scream was released by the dark entity as their hands made contact with each other and a dazzling light flooded the attic. As the shadows disappeared, the room brightened and became warm. Once again, Jacob's form faded, but not in the same way. There was a feeling of relief and tranquility.

Jacob said, "Thank you," in a grateful murmur. "Thank you for setting me free."

After saying that, he disappeared, leaving Helen by herself in the now-quiet attic. Knowing that she had helped find peace for another lost soul gave her a sense of satisfaction. While examining the attic, she couldn't shake the feeling that there were more mysteries to solve and more souls in need of her help.

Helen went back to the library in the days that followed, keen to find out more about the home and its troubled past. She poured hours into putting together the tale of the Hartwell family and the incidents that had brought them to ruin. She learned that Thomas Hartwell's experiments hurt his family and other community members.

Her labor was far from over, and she came to understand more and more. The home on Whispering Lane was a hub of paranormal activity and a location where the boundaries between other realities were blurry. Malevolent spirits had drawn to it, feeding off the anguish and terror of the people who had lived there.

Helen realized she was stuck in the house and couldn't go. She needed to discover a method to purify it entirely, to permanently shut the door that Thomas Hartwell had opened. Although it would be a risky undertaking, she felt obligated to shield others from the atrocities she had experienced.

After gathering her notes, Helen went back inside to be ready for the big showdown. She was aware that she had to locate the location of Thomas Hartwell's most potent rituals, which was the source of the dark energy. Most likely, it was concealed in a room or chamber that had gone unnoticed throughout the home.

She was lured to the basement as she looked around the home. It was a wet, shadowy space full of antique tools and misplaced artifacts. With caution, she advanced, creating unsettling shadows on the walls with her flashlight. She discovered a little entrance in the far corner of the basement, just visible behind a pile of discarded boxes.

She forced the door open after exerting some force, even though it was locked. Inside, there was a little stairway that descended into the shadows. With her heart thumping in her chest, she lowered herself carefully. She descended to the bottom and discovered a secret room with odd marks and symbols all over the walls.

An altar covered in dried blood stood in the middle of the room. This location was the epicenter of the dark energy that had afflicted the mansion, as well as the site of Thomas Hartwell's most risky experiments. Helen realized that in order to permanently seal the portal and drive out the evil spirits, she would need to carry out a powerful cleaning ceremony.

She prepared the room by arranging salt to act as a barrier and placing lights in a circle around the altar. She took the locket, which represented the love and grief of the Hartwell family, and set it on the altar. She inhaled deeply and started chanting the new phrases she had learned, pleading with the spirits to hear her request.

Tension filled the air, and the shadows surrounding her seemed to spring to life, writhing and twisting. Once again, the evil force reared its head, threatening to devour her. However, Helen had a strong will and an unwavering determination.

The dark presence was growling with rage as she chanted, and the shadows started to fade. A last, loud scream was released by the malignant power as the room filled with a bright light. As the shadows disappeared, the room brightened and became warm.

Helen knew she had done it, and she felt a wave of calm wash over her. The doorway closed, the dark presence vanished, and the Whispering Lane home was at last free of its sinister history.

Helen felt relieved and like a success as she stood in the suddenly quiet room. The restless ghosts that had tormented the home had found peace once she had fought the darkness and triumphed. However, she was aware that her task was not finished. Her assistance is needed for other locations and ghosts.

With a fresh sense of purpose, she prepared herself to take on whatever obstacles awaited her as she left the home on Whispering Lane. She had found her calling—a route that would take her on exciting new escapades and solve intriguing mysteries. She also knew that she would always remember the lessons she had learned and the souls she had freed as she turned to go.

Chapter 4

Shadows of Doubt

The Whispering Lane home seemed to be breathing better now that the wailing screams of imprisoned ghosts were no longer resonating through its walls. Although Helen had managed to bring some calm to the haunted house, she had also shown a restless side to herself. The secrets hidden in the ancient Victorian home were much greater than the puzzles she had solved, and she couldn't get rid of the notion that there was still more to learn.

Helen hesitated a little as she got ready to leave the house. A persistent uncertainty had crept into her thoughts, saying that she still had work to do. She decided to make one last visit to the residence in an effort to find closure.

Taking Another Look at the House

Once again, Helen found herself at the base of the opulent staircase—the very spot where her trip had started. Now the home felt different—almost pleasant, less oppressive. She headed toward the attic, where the ghost of young Jacob had appeared. With its worn-out furnishings and lost memories, the attic had become just another average room. But a shiver went down her spine as she stood there. There was still a problem.

In an attempt to dispel her misgivings, Helen decided to visit the local library once again. Mrs. Whitaker, the kind elderly librarian who had previously assisted her, welcomed her.

"Back again, Helen?" With her eyes sparkling with excitement, Mrs. Whitaker inquired.

Yes, Mrs Whitaker. I can't get rid of the sensation that I'm missing something. Do you possess any other documents pertaining to the Hartwell family or the Whispering Lane home?"

Mrs. Whitaker's face became grave. Without a doubt, the Hartwells were a problematic family. However, there is one record that I haven't yet shown you. It is an assortment of letters and journals written by Thomas Hartwell's wife, Elizabeth Hartwell. They might provide some insight into the actual events."

Helen trailed after Mrs. Whitaker into the archive room, where she was given an ancient leather-bound journal and a dusty box containing old letters. She took a seat at a table close by and started to read.

The letters, which were sent to Elizabeth's sister Margaret, described a troubled household. Elizabeth wrote about her concerns for their children and Thomas's developing preoccupation with the occult. She described unexplained happenings in the home, such as shadows moving on their own, whispering at night, and an increasing feeling of dread permeating every space.

One letter stuck out; it was dated not long before Emily passed away. Elizabeth described a shadowy apparition that materialized during Thomas's rites and seemed to follow him. She was afraid that Thomas had allowed something evil to enter their house by creating a portal to another world.

Helen continued to read and learned that while Elizabeth had attempted to intervene, Thomas had given in to his fixation. Helen was struck with sadness for the lady who had made such a valiant effort to shield her family after reading the last letters, which were full of desperation and hopelessness.

Elizabeth's journal revealed even more details about the sad history of the family. She wrote about how much she loved her kids and how afraid she was of losing them. She described the effects of Thomas's experiments on their family in detail. Elizabeth's descriptions of their last days in the journal became more and more desperate.

In one of her journal entries, Elizabeth described seeing a black figure standing over Emily's bed and talking in her ear. She begged Thomas to cease his experiments because she thought the figure was attempting to steal Emily. But Thomas had gone too far, too insane in his desperation to raise Emily from the grave.

The day Emily passed away, the last entry was made. Elizabeth spoke of her children's screaming, the turmoil and horror that had taken over the home, and her overpowering feeling of dread. She wrote about her last encounter with Thomas, in which she attempted to destroy the items he was using for his rituals. However, it was too late—the shadowy figure had already established itself.

Helen felt a wave of anxiety come over her as she closed the journal. Elizabeth had reported a black presence that felt uncannily familiar. It dawned on her that she had come across the same being while performing her ceremonies to release the spirits. There were still shadows in the house's corners, ones that had tormented the Hartwell family.

Helen went back to her home on Whispering Lane, determined to finally put an end to the gloom. Faced with the creature, she knew she had to drive it out of the house and ensure it never hurt anyone again.

Helen got ready for the ceremony by getting the things she would need, such as salt, candles, and Emily's locket. She formed a protective circle in the attic, the site of Thomas's most potent rites. The room felt colder, and the shadows seemed to draw in about her as she lit the candles.

She inhaled deeply and started chanting the phrases she had picked up from Elizabeth's journal. Tension filled the air as the shadows twisted and writhed, creating the appearance of a towering, dark person. It was a powerful presence—a dark energy that appeared to drain the room's light itself.

"Show yourself!" Fear overtook Helen, yet she still spoke with a calm voice. "I am aware of your identity and your past actions. It's time to go from here and never come back."

The shadowy silhouette approached, its eyes gleaming with evil intent. Even though Helen was overcome by a wave of darkness, she persisted in the chant, her voice becoming louder and her will unwavering. As the shadows started to fade, she was able to make out Thomas Hartwell's silhouette standing in the middle of the circle.

"Thomas, this is your last day here," Helen firmly said. "You must leave this place and take your darkness with you."

Though Thomas's figure bellowed with rage, Helen remained unwavering in her commitment. As she extended her hand, the figure retreated, its appearance starting to fade. A bright light flooded the room as the shadows twisted and writhed.

As the light faded, the apparition vanished, and the room became bright and warm. Helen knew she had done it, and she felt a wave of calm wash over her. The doorway closed, the dark presence vanished, and the Whispering Lane home was at last free of its sinister history.

Helen meticulously recorded her experiences in the days that followed. She wrote about the Hartwell family, the evil force that had befallen them, and the ceremonies she had carried out to drive it away. Her second book, a suspenseful story about haunted buildings and ghostly remnants of the past, was built on the notes and observations she made.

More than anything, Helen thought that the narrative would bring her readers to tears and provide her with a feeling of closure. The Whispering Lane mansion was no longer a source of terror and agony. Now that the evil force had been driven out, it served as a symbol of the strength of hope and the resiliency of the human spirit.

Feeling grateful and at ease, she made one more visit to the home. She placed the locket on the mantelpiece as a reminder of Emily's presence and their eternal love. As she left, the sun was setting, bathing the home in a warm light. The gentle rustling of leaves in the air had replaced the whispering. As a memento of her journey and the individuals she had impacted, Helen knew the home would always have a particular place in her heart.

Helen had changed in unexpected ways as a result of her experiences at the Whispering Lane mansion. Unbeknownst to her, she had found a power inside herself: a will to find the truth and provide comfort to those who had suffered. Despite the risks and uncertainty of the adventure, she had come out stronger and more resilient.

She was pleased with herself as she settled down to write the last chapter of her book. Readers would be moved, as she had been, by the tale of the Hartwell family's hardships and final serenity. She knew that there were still mysteries to solve and more ghosts to help find peace, so her mission was not yet complete. She knew that she had changed things; therefore, for the time being, she was happy.

She no longer carried the shadows of uncertainty; instead, she was filled with clarity and a feeling of purpose. Helen eagerly anticipated the mysteries and experiences that were ahead of her. She was sure she could overcome any obstacles with the same willpower that got her through the dark.

She was at peace, and so was the home on Whispering Lane.

Chapter 5

Dark Waters

As the sun set, Whispering Lane was covered with lengthy shadows. Helen stood at the property's edge, looking out over the darkened countryside. Behind her, the mansion loomed, quiet and still. Even though she had already discovered so much, she couldn't shake the feeling that she was missing something. She sensed there was more to the narrative—a darker, deeper reality that she had not yet discovered, even if the evil spirit she had faced in the attic had been defeated.

The morning after her last encounter with the shadowy figure, Helen was called to the local library by Mrs. Whitaker. Mrs. Whitaker replied, her voice laced with anxiety, "Helen, dear, I believe there's something you should see." " We just received some new donations that included Hartwell family records. "They mention a lake that's close to the land. It may be important to you, in my opinion."

Helen's interest was aroused. After expressing her gratitude to Mrs. Whitaker, she hurried to the library. Mrs. Whitaker welcomed her with an assortment of antiquated maps and a leather-bound notebook that had previously belonged to Thomas Hartwell. With much anticipation, Helen accepted the objects and found a peaceful area to study them.

The Hartwell estate's layout was shown on the maps, along with a little, secret lake tucked away in the dense forest. It was not far from the home, but none of the documents she had previously discovered had ever revealed their presence. Notes on the lake were recorded in great detail in the diary, in Thomas Hartwell's exacting writing. He had referred to it as "Lake Datura" and depicted it as a stronghold where the boundaries between dimensions were blurry.

With curiosity and a hint of caution, Helen decided to go to the lake. She filled a little satchel with necessities, including her notepad, a flashlight, and a few charms she'd picked up for protection while researching. The air became chilly, and the trees seemed to enclose her as she continued into the woods. She continued, despite the hazardous and overgrown route, because she felt a strong sense of urgency.

It seemed like hours before she made it to the lake's edge. The water was still and black, mirroring the thick, overhanging forest canopy. There was a palpable quietness all around, only sometimes disturbed by the sound of leaves rustling. As Helen moved closer to the water's edge, a shudder went down her spine.

A sharp chill blew through the air as she bent to fill a vial with water from the lake. When Helen glanced up, she saw someone standing on the other side of the beach. She was a woman with an ethereal and transparent body. The spectral person exuded grief and was dressed in long, flowing clothing. Elizabeth Hartwell was instantly recognizable to Helen because of the antique pictures in the home.

Whispering, "Elizabeth," Helen's voice faltered. "Why are you here?"

The spectral apparition did not say anything, yet something appeared to be spoken with her eyes. The ghost exuded a depressing and desperate feeling that overwhelmed Helen. Elizabeth gestured to the middle of the lake, where the surface seemed to be turbulent and undulating.

Helen recognized. Something was in the water, something related to the shadowy figure she had faced. With a jolt of resolve, she nodded in Elizabeth's direction. "I'll locate it," she pledged.

Helen undressed to reveal the truth, and she braved the chilly, dark waters in her bathing suit. She felt a chill go through her every step, but she continued. She started to swim toward the lake's center as the water rapidly became deeper. She could sense the attraction of something strong under the surface, which was surprisingly serene.

She inhaled deeply and sank below the surface. In the dim light, she could only see the outline of something. The water was muddy and visibility was poor. She stretched out and grabbed the object as she swam further down, her lungs burning. It was a tiny, elaborate cage covered with silt and algae.

She experienced a wave of relief and dread when she emerged. Shivering from the cold, she swam back to the coast and got out of the sea. Elizabeth's ghost was still there, watching her closely. After setting the package down, Helen gingerly unwrapped it.

A bundle of letters bound with a red ribbon, a tiny vial containing a black liquid, and a locket were among the weird objects she discovered within. Thomas Hartwell wrote the letters himself, describing his investigations and the customs he had followed at the lake. He had utilized the lake's power in his frantic efforts to bring Emily back because he thought its dark waters held the answer to crossing the gap between life and death.

Helen began to feel more and more apprehensive as she read the letters. She had no idea how insane and deadly Thomas's experiments had been. Using the lake's capacity to call out and manipulate spirits, he carried out sinister rites. The letters mentioned a last ceremony that called for a significant sacrifice and finally brought him and Elizabeth to ruin.

Elizabeth's soul approached, remorse and anguish shining in her eyes. Now Helen knew. Thomas's last desperate ritual resulted in the dark presence she had faced in the home. He had let a malicious force enter their planet by creating a portal to another dimension. Though it was too late, Elizabeth had attempted to stop him.

Helen was aware that she had to permanently drive the creature out by sealing the gateway. After taking everything out of the box, she headed back towards home. The land was covered in deep shadows as the sun began to set. She felt urgency because she knew she had to move quickly.

She made a fresh protective circle in the attic and positioned the contents of the box within. Using the phrases she had acquired from Elizabeth's diaries and Thomas's letters, she lit candles and started to chant. Tension filled the air, and the room's shadows seemed to spring to life.

As she sang, the black presence materialized, whirling about her in a maelstrom of whispers and shadows. Although Helen experienced a rush of terror, she ignored it and concentrated on the ceremony. She raised the locket and black liquid vial, channeling the water's power.

The black entity growled with rage, but Helen remained steadfast in her vow. As she resumed the chant, her voice became louder with every phrase. She recognized the towering, dark figure formed by the writhing and twisting shadows as the one she had seen before.

"Thomas Hartwell," she said, her tone unwavering. "Your stay has now concluded. You have to carry this darkness with you and get out of here."

Thomas's shadowy form approached, his evil-looking eyes gleaming. Helen felt the power of the vial and locket flow toward her, and she aimed it toward the figure. With a cry of defiance, the black figure started to retreat from the shadows.

There was one more terrible scream, and then the room was full of bright light, and the shadows vanished. The gateway was closed, and the black entity had vanished. Helen knew she had done it, and she felt a wave of calm wash over her.

At last, the home on Whispering Lane was rid of its troubled history. With a sense of relaxation and satisfaction, Helen stood in the attic. The restless ghosts that had tormented the home had found peace once she had fought the darkness and triumphed. However, she was aware that her task was not finished. Her assistance is needed for other locations and ghosts.

She had a feeling of finality as she gathered her belongings and got ready to depart. She had ended the shadow that had followed the

Hartwell family and unearthed the truth about their sad history. The home on Whispering Lane was now a haven of tranquility, a symbol of the strength of hope and the resiliency of the human spirit.

With a fresh sense of purpose, Helen left the house prepared to take on whatever obstacles lay ahead. Even though she knew her trip was far from over, she felt satisfied that she had had an impact. She no longer carried the shadows of uncertainty; instead, she was filled with clarity and a feeling of purpose.

She was at peace, and so was the home on Whispering Lane. As she left, the sun was setting, bathing the home in a warm light. The gentle rustling of leaves in the air had replaced the whispering. As a memento of her journey and the individuals she had impacted, Helen knew the home would always have a particular place in her heart.

Helen meticulously recorded her experiences in the days that followed. Her second book, a suspenseful story about haunted buildings and ghostly remnants of the past, was built on the notes and observations she made. She was certain that the narrative would enthrall her readers, but more than anything, it gave her a feeling of finality. She was prepared to go on her adventure, wherever it would take her, having confronted the darkness and come out on top.

Chapter 6

The Mirror's Reflection

Helen Donovan believed that calm had finally been restored to the home on Whispering Lane. She had faced the eerie presence, learned of the Hartwell family's terrible past, and appeared to have driven the evil spirit from the house. However, as the days stretched into weeks, an unsettling thought crept into the back of her mind. The mansion seemed to be hiding one more mystery that was just waiting to be discovered.

The first sign appeared to be a recurring dream. In the master bedroom, Helen found herself standing in front of an elaborate full-length mirror. Only the mirror's opaque black surface showed her image. In the dream, as her fingertips touched the glass, a chilly, unsettling murmur would reverberate through the space, urging Helen to uncover the truth. Examine more closely."

The dream's vividness startled Helen, so she decided to look into it further. She had always been fascinated by the master bedroom mirror, with its ornate frame adorned with symbols and artistic motifs. It was an antique, most likely brought in by Thomas Hartwell himself. She studied the mirror's history and importance for many days, determined to learn its mysteries.

She learned from her investigation that the mirror was an antique with a sordid past rather than just a lovely item. Known by the moniker "Mirror of Zafira," it was made in the sixteenth century by a witch. Legend has it that Zafira bestowed strong enchantments on the mirror, enabling it to function as a conduit between realms. It was claimed that the mirror could disclose the innermost secrets of the person gazing into it, as well as the truth concealed beneath falsehoods.

Helen's pulse raced as she read the stories of people who had come across the mirror throughout the years. Many reported seeing ghosts, hearing phantom sounds, and even going missing. The more information she gathered, the more certain she was that the mirror held the secret to solving the last unsolved mystery surrounding the Hartwell family.

Helen decided it was time to face the mirror one evening, as the sun was setting and casting sweeping shadows over the space. With her pulse thumping in her chest, she shut the master bedroom door and stepped toward the mirror. One candle lit the room weakly, causing light to flicker across the mirror's surface.

She inhaled deeply, stepped in front of the mirror, and stared into it. Her reflection was all she could see at first, but as she concentrated, the glass started to shimmer and warp. "Helen, find the truth," the familiar voice said as it filled the room, sending shivers down her spine. Examine more closely."

She stretched out and touched the glass with a shaking palm. The room appeared to vanish in an instant, and she was left standing in a gloomy, black place. She was encircled by the faint echo of murmurs and an overpowering electricity in the air. She became aware that she was really in the mirror, not the master bedroom.

Helen moved ahead, leaving a trail of sound behind her. Before her, the shadows seemed to lift, exposing snippets of the past. She saw Thomas Hartwell, a shattered individual driven insane by despair. He was in front of the mirror, carrying out the sinister rite that let the evil forces loose in their world. His voice shook, and his eyes were empty as he recited spells, pleading for his daughter to come back.

Then she saw Elizabeth Hartwell's face, etched with dread and grief. She begged Thomas to quit, to give up his risky activities, but he was uncontrollably unreasonable. When the ceremony came to a head, a swirling mass of evil and darkness burst out of the mirror, revealing the creature. As the scene changed, Helen saw Thomas and Elizabeth have their terrible last encounter. The thing's presence intensified, consuming both of them as it fed on their rage and hopelessness.

Helen watched with tears in her eyes as the Hartwell family spiraled downhill into lunacy and hopelessness. She was aware of their sorrow's intensity and could feel their anxiety and agony. However, the murmurs encouraged her to go on and explore the mysteries behind the mirror in greater detail.

The murmurs became louder, and the shadows surrounding her got heavier as she continued. Despite her intense feeling of dread, she knew she had to do this. Finally, she arrived in the center of the shadows, and a tall, menacing figure emerged from the shadows.

When the apparition moved forward, Helen knew it was the same person who had haunted the home. Its voice was a deep, rumbling murmur, and its eyes flashed with a malignant radiance that said, "You seek the truth, Helen Donovan." You want to know what's on the other side of the curtain."

Helen said, her voice quivering, "I must know why. What prompted this to happen? What can I do to stop it?"

The thing's chuckle reverberated through the emptiness, a spooky noise that made her shudder. "The Hartwells served only as a tool. I was strengthened by their dread and sorrow, but you, Helen, were the one who really carried me through. You are confined to this location by your insatiable curiosity and need to learn the truth."

A twinge of remorse and terror gripped Helen. Her need to learn more had always motivated her, but now she worried whether she had unintentionally increased the entity's might. Her voice was hardly audible as she questioned, "What do you want from me?"

With a voice that seemed as though it were speaking directly to her, the entity's eyes went straight into hers, and she said, "I want freedom, which is what all creatures of evil seek. If you remove me from this mirror, I'll be free to go about your world and prey on other people's anxiety and hopelessness."

Helen's thoughts were racing. She couldn't allow the creature to go free and bring evil to the planet. However, how could she permanently destroy it? She remembered the protection charms and rituals she had studied over the years, and the solution came to her instantly.

Gathering all her bravery, Helen confronted the thing and started chanting the spells she had studied. Her remarks were full of will and determination as they came out of her mouth. In response to her enchantment's might, the darkness all around her started to squirm and contort in response to the might of her enchantment.

The object shrieked with rage, solidifying and defining its shape. It surged at her, but she held her position and kept her mind on the chant. As the spell reached its peak, the air crackled with electricity, and a dazzling light filled the space.

The creature let out one last, terrible cry before being dragged back into the mirror and having its shape melt into the glass. The shadows dipped, and Helen was back in the master bedroom, the mirror's surface opaque and black once more.

Helen, worn out but victorious, fell to the ground. She had fought through the night and emerged victorious. She and her home were free from the mirror's spell. Instead of whispering, there was a deep silence.

Helen took action in the days that followed to make sure the terrible past of the mirror would never be forgotten. After painstakingly documenting her encounters, she shared her discoveries with the town's historical organization and other scholars. After the mirror's charms were neutralized, it was carefully wrapped and put in a safe place.

Helen had a feeling of finality as she thought back on her trip. She had ended the evil entity's rule and unearthed the last remaining secrets of the Hartwell family. At last, she and the home on Whispering Lane were at peace.

Helen was transformed by her experiences at the Whispering Lane residence. Having overcome her worst anxieties, she was now stronger and more determined than before. Her insatiable curiosity and quest for knowledge had brought her into the dark, but they had also given her the willpower to face and conquer it.

Her second book was based on the Hartwell family's story and the mirror's sinister charms. She put herself fully into her writing, encapsulating her trip and the lessons she'd discovered. Many were drawn to the story of mystery, sorrow, and victory in "Silent Screams," which went on to become a bestseller.

Helen realized she had a lot more work ahead of her. There were other locations and tales that needed telling. Motivated by a feeling of duty and a desire to know the truth, she carried out further research. But she would always have a particular place in her heart for the home on Whispering Lane, wherever her travels brought her.

Helen stood at the property's edge, gazing over the renovated home years later. The home was now a beacon of hope and resilience, instead of a place of gloom and misery. It served as a symbol of the value of finding the truth and the strength of facing one's anxieties.

Helen felt content and proud as she looked around the house. She had confronted the darkness in the mirror and come out stronger. She was free of the ghosts of the past, filled with the realization that she had changed things.

She had seen the strength of optimism and the depths of sorrow in the mirror reflection. It had given her the courage to face the darkness and exposed the reality that was concealed by falsehoods. Ultimately, it had shown the way to her resolution and tranquility.

With confidence, prepared to take on whatever obstacles lay ahead, Helen turned and left. She was at peace, and so was the home on Whispering Lane.

Chapter 7

Footsteps in the Fog

The mist of early dawn enveloped Whispering Lane as if it were a cloak, obfuscating the boundaries between reality and transforming the well-known terrain into an eerie scene. With its former hauntings banished, the home stood placidly against the haze, its freshly discovered loveliness standing in sharp contrast to the memories of its history. But as Helen Donovan got closer to the property again, she had a dreadful sensation that something strange was moving in the thick mist.

Mrs. Whitaker had called Helen the night before. Mrs. Whitaker snapped over the phone, "Helen, I'm sorry to bother you so late, but I've come across something unusual." "The Hartwell estate is once again at issue." Something that defies our current understanding has been discovered. "Could you see us at the library in the morning?"

Helen agreed to see Mrs. Whitaker out of curiosity. As she navigated through the mist, her thoughts turned back to the incidents from her earlier research. Though it had seemed serene, the mansion had been a site of secrets and tragedies, and she knew from experience that old mysteries had a way of coming back to haunt you.

Helen was met by Mrs. Whitaker when she arrived at the library, and she was shown to a back room containing historical papers and archives.

"Helen, please look at this," Mrs. Whitaker said, handing her a ledger with a leather cover. "We've recently uncovered a series of letters and documents that suggest something more may have happened at the estate, something connected to the fog."

Helen grabbed the ledger and started going through the paperwork. These were scrawled notes, written in a hurry, full of cryptic allusions to the fog that shrouded the property at different periods of the year. Many disappearances that had happened decades before the Hartwell family came to Whispering Lane were described in the letters.

Among the letters, one dated 1923 jumped out:

"Fog is a curtain, not simply a weather condition." It hides the real nature of what is waiting beyond. I've heard whispers about old things and seen shadows moving through the mist. Take caution—those who go too far risk being permanently lost.

Helen was not acquainted with Eleanor Hughes, the person who signed the letter. She realized she needed to comprehend the fog, so she made a point to look into it further. The more she learned, the more it appeared that the fog was more than just a product of the weather; it could play a major role in the estate's darker past.

Helen decided to spend some time in the fog the following day, touring the grounds. Carrying a torch, a notepad, and a feeling of dread, she made her way through the thick forests and overgrown trails around the house.

Her flashlight's beam sliced through the dense mist as she descended more into the fog, creating unsettling shadows on the trees. The universe seemed to contract and contort around her, and the only sounds breaking the stillness were the infrequent rustling of leaves and the far-off cry of a bird. Occasionally, she believed she heard footsteps like her own, but upon turning around, she found no one.

Helen kept searching, heading toward the lake that served as the main target of her earlier research. The fog overhangs the lake, creating an impenetrable gray mirror on its surface. She got a queasy feeling, like there was something sinister lurking in the water that she had not yet discovered.

The mists parted just as she was standing at the lake's edge, showing a person on the far side. It was a woman in a period gown, her face hidden by the mist. As Helen got closer to the stranger, her pulse raced.

"Hello?" Helen yelled, her voice shaking slightly. "Are you lost?"

Slowly, the woman's face emerged from behind her head. It was none other than Eleanor Hughes, the same mysterious letter writer. Her eyes were filled with a combination of resignation and hopelessness, and her face was one of intense melancholy.

Eleanor remarked, "You must be Helen Donovan," her voice resonating oddly through the mist. "I've been waiting for you."

It was evident how shocked and confused Helen was. "You are Hughes Eleanor. How do you feel about being here? You wrote those letters, but why?"

With a sigh, Eleanor looked away. "Fog is more than simply a product of the weather. It serves as a wall between our world and another." It is my responsibility as a kind of guardian to make sure the curtain between worlds doesn't break."

With decades of suffering in her voice, Eleanor started to tell her tale. "My family and I lived here on Whispering Lane at the beginning of the 20th century." We were scholars, exploring old writings and customs. We learned that the fog had a protective function, preventing evil forces from passing through."

She hesitated as the faint glow from Helen's flashlight reflected in her eyes. But we were mistaken that fateful night. We carried out our ritual to increase our understanding, unaware that it would erode the border. That night, individuals began to disappear, and shadows began to appear from the other side. I attempted to stop the break with my family, but it was too late. I was left here, confined to the mist, attempting to save others from suffering the same fate."

Helen paid attention, taking in the seriousness of Eleanor's remarks. "Therefore, the fog is a barrier." So why does it continue to exist? And how might it be resolved?"

Eleanor gave a sad nod. "The breach was never completely fixed, which is why the fog continues. Because the ceremony we attempted was not complete, the shadows are still present in our reality and continue to feed on the hopelessness and terror they instill. You have to finish the ritual that was left undone in order to seal the gap. However, heed this warning: The shadows are strong and will attempt to stop you."

Helen consented to assist Eleanor in finishing the ceremony because she was determined to dispel the lingering gloom. Eleanor gave her a series of instructions detailing what needed to be done to seal the break and restore the barrier. A bottle of holy water from the lake, an old charm, and a unique incantation were needed for the ceremony.

Helen went back inside and collected everything she needed. The air in the home seemed to vibrate with expectancy, and the mood was strained. She prepared the ceremonial area in the attic, where she had previously encountered a shadowy figure. The feeling of urgency increased as the fog outside became heavier.

Helen went over the directions Eleanor had given her as she got ready for the ceremony. The ritual water was to be used to purify the area, the charm was to be positioned in the middle of the circle, and the incantation was to be chanted with steadfast concentration.

She sprayed the holy water and lit candles around the circle, watching as the water reflected light into the dark chamber. After placing the charm with precision, Helen inhaled deeply and braced herself for the task at hand.

As soon as Helen started the incantation, the fog outside seemed to become thicker and more obstructive. Her statements were delivered with such force that the whole room felt their impact. The attic's shadows seemed to come to life, whirling and contorting in reaction to the ceremony.

The attic's shadows became darker and more pronounced as Helen chanted, eventually forming into grotesque shapes. The room's temperature fell, and growls and murmurs filled the air. With palpable evil energy, the shadows surged at Helen.

Even though Helen's heart was racing, she was determined to finish the spell. She concentrated on the charm, channeling the energy of the ceremony through it. Although the shadows retaliated, exerting their might against the ritual's power, Helen's determination did not waver.

The chamber was a battlefield of light and dark, the force of the ritual colliding with the evil of the shadows. Helen experienced physical and mental distress as a result of the ceremony. Nevertheless, she persisted because she understood that Whispering Lane's future and harmony between realms rested on her shoulders.

A bright light enveloped the chamber as the ceremony came to a close. The shadows drew back, their shapes vanishing into nothingness. The dense darkness above the estate started to dissipate as the fog outside started to disperse. When the gap was eventually sealed, a feeling of peace and relief permeated the air.

Helen, worn out but victorious, fell to the ground. The fog had dissipated, and the shadows had vanished. The malice that had been plaguing the home on Whispering Lane for so long had finally gone.

Helen gave herself some time to think back on her experiences in the days that followed. The cloud that had previously covered the home in obscurity had cleared, and it was back to its former splendor. The rite had been successful, and the world's equilibrium had been restored.

Motivated by the insights and understanding she had acquired throughout her tenure at Whispering Lane, Helen persisted in her investigative work. Her book, "Silent Screams," sprang to fame as readers were enthralled with the story of bravery, mystery, and victory.

Helen had a profound feeling of satisfaction as she reflected on her adventure. She had triumphed against the darkness, restoring harmony to the home and its turbulent history. She had finally uncovered the last remaining mysteries of Whispering Lane, and now she was prepared to take on any obstacles that lay ahead.

She would always carry with her the legacy of Whispering Lane, a testament to the strength of bravery and tenacity in the face of adversity. Helen also understood that the lessons she had gained from the light and the shadows would serve as a guide for her future exploration of knowledge and the truth.

Chapter 8

Secrets of the Old Cemetery

Whispering Lane's silence appeared to have settled into a restless calm. The estate was now clear and almost too tranquil, the fog that had earlier engulfed it having lifted. Now that it was rid of the ghosts of the past, the mansion stood for forgiveness and fresh beginnings. However, Helen Donovan started to feel uneasy again as she thought back on what had happened.

While visiting the local history organization, Helen came across a mention of the ancient cemetery outside of town. She had never realized how closely the overgrown and mostly forgotten cemetery was connected to the Hartwell family. An ancient ledger discovered in the archives described the cemetery's history and alluded to strange incidents relating to it.

The ledger described an odd connection between the cemetery and a slew of unexplained deaths and disappearances that had befallen the town in the early 1900s. The more she read, Helen began to believe that this cemetery may contain the key to unlocking a new chapter in the Hartwell mystery, one that would shed light on yet another terrible aspect of Whispering Lane's past.

One cool fall morning, Helen's inquiry took her to the ancient graveyard. The clear, light blue sky and cool air contrasted with the graveyard's gloomy atmosphere. Perched on a hillside just beyond the town, the wrought iron gate was half-hidden by spreading ivy and rust. The only noises in the silent, melancholy cemetery were the rustling of leaves and the far-off chirping of birds.

Helen saw the cemetery's ruinous condition as she pulled open the creaking gate. Some of the gravestones were tilted at strange angles and were broken and weathered. The weeds had strangled the once-tidy paths, and the grass had become overgrown. The cemetery itself seemed to be holding its breath, waiting for something—or someone—despite its state of ruin. There was something strangely alluring about the location.

With caution, Helen made her way over the uneven terrain as she started her investigation, noting the different gravestones. While many of the names were unknown, Eleanor Hughes' name jumped out. The name fit the lady who'd been lost in the mist, but this Eleanor Hughes was not the one from the letters; in fact, it was her mother, buried here long before the Hartwells came.

Helen was attracted to a very ancient and worn headstone as she carried on with her quest. She recognized the name inscribed on it: Thomas Hartwell. The findings were both surprising and fascinating. Thomas Hartwell's family may have had a role in the cemetery's past, according to the historical society's ledger, but his burial was not mentioned.

She squatted down next to the tombstone and cleared the rubble. Though hardly readable, the inscription verified her suspicions: Thomas Hartwell had been buried here, far away from the estate. This prompted a lot of inquiries. What was the reason for Thomas Hartwell's interment at a completely forgotten cemetery? And why had this not been brought up in any of the earlier studies?

A slight shuffling sound behind her sent Helen a shiver down her spine and broke her reverie. When she turned around, nobody was there. She pushed the uneasy sensation away and carried on with her research, but she couldn't shake the feeling that she was being watched.

Helen looked for hours before finding an overgrown trail that went to a remote spot at the cemetery's edge. The trail was almost completely obscured by a dense canopy of entwined vines and fallen leaves. Helen, intrigued, pushed her way through the undergrowth and came out into a little clearing.

An ancient, dilapidated tomb stood in the middle of the clearing. A big, fallen tree partly obstructed the entry, and moss coated the stone façade. Given its architecture, the mausoleum appeared older than other cemetery buildings. Helen was filled with fear and excitement as she walked up to the tomb, her pulse pounding.

It took Helen a long time to move the debris out of the entryway. The thick stone door groaned open to show a musty, gloomy chamber. After shining her flashlight into the shadows, she entered.

The tomb was cluttered with dust and spiderwebs. There were alcoves all over the walls, each holding a fading plaque and sometimes skeletal bones. Helen saw an elaborate sarcophagus at the far end of the mausoleum. Its surface was finely engraved with symbols she knew from her previous studies; they were the identical symbols Eleanor Hughes had used in her rituals.

Helen heard a faint, melancholy sound that seemed like it was coming from the shadows as she drew closer to the tomb and felt a breath of frigid air. The murmur intensified, creating barely audible syllables. "Watch out for the shadows; they're not who they seem."

Helen was having trouble breathing. When she had previously interacted with the paranormal aspects of the home, she had heard whispers that sounded similar. But this was different—more urgent, more desperate.

Helen opened the tomb gingerly and with some fear. She discovered a skeleton dressed in deteriorated finery inside. She first thought it was just another burial until she saw something strange: a little, leather-bound diary that the corpse was holding tightly.

Helen took the diary out with care and started to read. The last days of the individual buried in the sarcophagus were described in the notes, which were written in a weak, frantic hand. According to the diary, the person was really one of Thomas Hartwell's acquaintances who had been heavily engaged in the dark rites, not Thomas Hartwell, as she had first thought.

The notes described a state of anxiety, betrayal, and a last-ditch effort to seal the hole the rituals had created. The author spoke about a secret room under the graveyard, where the last rituals had to be carried out in order to stifle the evil energy that had been let loose.

Equipped with the recently discovered details from the diary, Helen set out to find the concealed room that was referenced there. The journal entries explained a labyrinth of underground passageways and tunnels that led to a last resting spot where the ritual might be finished.

Helen carefully followed the instructions, utilizing her gut feelings and the mysterious hints from the diary to help her explore the cemetery grounds. Under a massive, rotting oak tree, she found an opening to a tunnel. She struggled through the doorway and dropped down into the shadows.

The air was heavy with the smell of decay, and the tunnels were small and wet. Helen navigated the twisting hallways, creating unsettling shadows on the walls with her flashlight. The environment became more oppressive the further she descended. The murmurs became more insistent, as if the walls were trying to communicate with her.

She eventually came to a room at the tunnel's terminus. The room was crammed with ceremonial items and antiquated relics, some of which fit the descriptions found in Eleanor Hughes' notes. A massive stone altar covered with fading symbols and inscriptions stood in the middle of the room.

Helen stepped up to the altar and took in her surroundings. The room appears to be the last location mentioned in the ceremony logbook. It was obvious that here was the location where the breach needed to be permanently sealed.

Helen knew performing the ritual was risky, but she knew it was necessary to protect the estate and community. She went into the room and took out the necessary supplies for the ceremony, which included a ceremonial knife, old charms, and a vial of holy water.

Now that everything was ready, Helen started the ceremony. The atmosphere was unsettling, yet she spoke clearly and steadily as she recounted the incantations from the notebook. As she worked, the whispering in the room became louder, almost as if in response to the ceremony, and the symbols on the altar started to light dimly.

The room's shadows formed ominous forms and swirled around Helen as if they were alive. They danced erratically, their figures altering as they tried to sabotage the ceremony. However, Helen didn't waver and gave the rite her whole attention.

As the ceremony neared its peak, electricity crackled through the air. The ceremony's energy caused the shadows to retreat, diminishing their strength. The murmurs became a chorus of agonized screams as the symbols on the altar burst into brilliant light.

With one last burst of energy, Helen finished the ceremony. The altar's light filled the room, driving the darkness away and permanently closing the opening. The stifling air parted, and quietness descended over the apartment.

Helen came out of the secret room exhausted but relieved, and she headed back to the graveyard. A clear sky and a feeling of peace had replaced the fog that had earlier shrouded the estate. It seems that the cemetery has also been cleansed of any remaining evil.

Helen took a moment to consider what had happened. The last missing piece of the jigsaw, which would have sealed the gap and revealed the history buried away, had been found in the ancient graveyard. The shadows had vanished when the rite was finished.

Helen had a strong feeling of closure as she walked out of the graveyard. The gloom that had afflicted the estate had finally disappeared, and the secrets of Whispering Lane had been revealed. The town, the cemetery, and the home on Whispering Lane were free of the evil spirits that had previously controlled them.

Following their time at Whispering Lane, Helen's experiences served as the basis for her most recent novel, "Silent Screams." The excursion around the estate and cemetery was described in full in the book, which also captured the spirit of the mystery and the successful conclusion.

Whispering Lane eventually reverted to its previous state of affairs. With its tragic history finally put to rest, the estate is now a symbol of resiliency and restoration. Although Helen carried on with her career as an investigator, she would always be connected to Whispering Lane and its mysteries.

Looking back on her trip, Helen had a deep feeling of achievement. Whispering Lane was no longer plagued by shadows, and the ghosts of the past had vanished. Finding the truth and reestablishing equilibrium had been made possible in large part by the ancient cemetery with its mysteries and hidden rooms.

Whispering Lane left behind a legacy of bravery, tenacity, and an unwavering pursuit of the truth. Helen's experience served as an example of the strength that comes from fighting adversity and the power of perseverance. She also took with her the knowledge she had gained from the light and the darkness, prepared to take on any obstacles that stood in her way.

Chapter 9

The Haunting Melody

Since Helen Donovan's previous visit, a lot has changed at the Whispering Lane residence. It was once a place of mystery and gloom, but today it stands as a symbol of how past tragedies have been put to rest. Still, the peace was a mirage. The mansion possessed mysteries that were yet undiscovered, despite its tastefully renovated rooms and quiet passageways.

When Helen unexpectedly got a parcel at her workplace, the narrative started again. The package was covered in brown paper and was plain and straightforward. There was a small, elaborate music box inside. It was really well made, and although it was old, it seemed to have been polished lately. The music box was accompanied by a quivering, hurriedly scrawled message that said, "Helen, I hope you receive this in time." I'm not sure why this music box is the way it is. I've had it for years, but it belongs to the Hartwell family. Since I brought it home, it has been acting strangely. I think it has something to do with Whispering Lane's previous atrocities. Please look into this. Rebecca, a nearby antique dealer,

Helen felt her interest peak. Rebecca, a nearby antique merchant, had already given her many clues. She chose to go see Rebecca in order to learn more about the music box's background.

Rebecca's store was a charming, comfortable area with a large selection of antiques, each with a unique history. The aroma of polished metal and ancient wood filled the air. Rebecca welcomed Helen with warmth as she entered, but there was a tinge of nervousness in her eyes.

Rebecca remarked, "Helen, I'm glad you could come," and she led Helen to a little back room where the music box had been stored. "Ever since I acquired this music box, it has caused me discomfort."

Helen took a careful look at the music box. It was exquisitely made, with fine engravings that showed pictures of tranquil landscapes and lovely flower designs. There was a little pocket on the side that held the key. Helen gently wound the key and raised the lid with Rebecca's consent.

A quiet, mournful song that gave the place an eerie atmosphere started to play from the music box. The melodies were lovely, yet there was a hint of melancholy that seemed to speak directly to Helen.

Rebecca looked on anxiously. The business has seen unusual happenings ever since I began playing it. I've experienced dreams where things move by themselves. I used to believe it was all in my head, but now I'm not so sure.

Helen's thoughts were racing. The tune was uncannily familiar; it reminded her of the noises and murmurs she had heard during her earlier research. She believed that the music box could help her learn more about the disruptions at Whispering Lane, which may be possible with the help of the music box.

Resolved to find out where the music box came from, Helen brought it back to her study. The next several days were spent learning about its past. The music box's elaborate design and the tune it played indicated that it was constructed in the late 19th century, which is when many of the events she had looked into took place.

According to her research, the Hartwell family had previously owned a music box. It was a gift from Edward Winslow, a prominent figure in the town's history and close family friend. Winslow was linked to the eerie rites carried out at the estate and was well-known for his interest in the occult.

Winslow had been actively engaged in efforts to make contact with the afterlife, according to further research. The music box was one of the numerous gadgets he was supposed to have made to let people communicate with the dead. This was a disturbing realization. If the music box does indeed serve as a medium for communication with the hereafter, it may possibly account for the peculiar happenings at Rebecca's store and Whispering Lane.

Helen chose to play the music box in the same location where the disruptions had happened since she was determined to learn more. She went back to the Hartwell estate and utilized one of the empty rooms to create a controlled atmosphere. Helen placed the music box gently on a table and started to play the tune once again.

Aside from the music, the place was quiet. Helen felt the mood shift as the notes filled the room. The light coming in through the windows wavered, and the temperature appeared to plummet. The music seemed to make the shadows on the walls dance and change.

A shiver went down Helen's spine. Something that had been hiding in the estate's shadows was being revealed by the tune. She listened intently, searching for any other noises or patterns that might provide further information.

Helen began to hear small murmurs that blended in with the music as it played. They were too quiet to hear the regrettable tone. It seemed as though the house was communicating via the music box, since the whispers appeared to originate from the walls themselves.

Helen focused on the murmurs, attempting to interpret their meaning. The murmurs eventually came together to form a clear message after a few minutes:

"Aid us... We're ensnared. the key, the melody, and so on.

Although the message was disjointed, it was nevertheless obvious enough to make the urgency evident. The spirits were stuck and in need of assistance. There was a connection between the music and their situation, and the key may provide the answer.

Helen made the decision to learn more about the Hartwell family's past and how they were related to Edward Winslow. She discovered that

Winslow had been fixated on figuring out how to connect the living and the dead. His effort to establish communication with the hereafter was the music box, with its eerie tune.

Helen went back to the secret room she had found in the ancient graveyard with her newfound insight. She thought the room could provide further hints about the souls imprisoned by the sinister rituals and the music box.

Helen had not spotted the little, concealed compartment on the wall until she stepped into the room. She opened it cautiously and discovered an ancient, worn diary inside. Edward Winslow kept a notebook in which he recorded his experiences interacting with the afterlife.

Per the diary, Winslow made the music box to communicate with ghosts. A set of rites intended to create a portal to the spirit realm were also discussed. But something had gone awry during the ceremonies, leaving the spirits suspended in midair.

According to the diary, the only way to free them was to perform the ceremony and use the music box as a conduit to help the imprisoned souls cross over. Complete directions for carrying out the ceremony, including the usage of certain symbols and incantations, were included in the diary.

Equipped with the insights gained from Winslow's notebook, Helen proceeded to get ready for the ceremony. She collected the essentials—the music box, candles, and unique symbols. As instructed, she meticulously set up the ceremonial area in the concealed room.

With candles set in a circle and symbols painted on the floor, the room was converted into a hallowed area. With its eerie song quietly playing in the background, the music box was positioned in the middle. Helen was nervous and excited at the same time as she got ready to carry out the ceremony.

As she began, the room's mood became electric. The murmurs appeared to become louder, and the shadows on the walls seemed to get deeper. With unwavering conviction, Helen recited the incantations from the diary as she concentrated on the ceremony.

Throughout the ceremony, the music box's song flowed through, its notes harmonizing with the atmosphere in the room. As the shadows started to take shape, spectral forms emerged that seemed to reach out and touch the music box. The song elicited responses from the ghosts, drawing them in like a beacon.

The energy in the room swelled as the ceremony reached its peak. Now that they were completely visible, the spirits materialized into transparent, ethereal forms. There were looks of pain and desire on their cheeks. They appeared to be reaching out to grab something that was out of reach.

Helen carried on the ceremony, using the music box's melody to guide the spirits. The ghosts seemed lighter, their shapes vanishing into the air as the energy in the room grew stronger. The music continued—a melancholic, gentle song that made their journey seem less difficult.

There was a feeling of quiet and harmony in the room as the ceremony came to an end. The murmuring subsided into silence as the shadows moved away. Now that the spirits were free, their imprisoned souls could finally go on.

Helen, relieved yet fatigued, fell to the ground. The music box's eerie tune had succeeded in sending the ghosts beyond the threshold. The room exuded a calm aura that had previously been associated with gloom and hopelessness.

The unrest at Whispering Lane subsided in the days that followed. The music box was taken back to its resting position inside the estate, now quiet. After the imprisoned souls were released, the home remained a symbol of rebirth and reconciliation.

Helen had closed a major chapter in Whispering Lane's history with her study of the music box and the ghosts. The eerie tune had served as a medium for communication that finally resulted in the spirits' release, serving as both a curse and a gift.

Helen wrote about her experiences in her most recent book chapter, "Silent Screams." Discovering the mystery, bravery, and unwavering pursuit of truth that surround the music box, as well as its relationship to the ghosts of Whispering Lane, has become an enthralling tale.

Helen had a profound feeling of satisfaction as she thought back on her adventure. The release of the spirits signaled the conclusion of a long and difficult inquiry, in which the music box had been instrumental in revealing the last missing parts of the jigsaw.

The eerie tune would live on in Whispering Lane's past, a testament to the strength of bravery and tenacity in the face of adversity. Helen realized that her trip was far from over as she carried on with her task. The teachings of the light and the shadows served as constant guidance in the never-ending search for knowledge and truth.

Chapter 10

Into the Abyss

At last, the once-unstable home on Whispering Lane had embraced a precarious serenity. The estate now stood as a symbol of both resolution and renewal; the ghosts of previous atrocities were silenced. At a crossroads, Helen Donovan, the tenacious detective who had solved the secrets surrounding the Hartwell inheritance, found herself. Her study had revealed many dark secrets that had come to light as a result of her study, but there was an uneasy feeling that not all of them had.

One evening, Helen received another mysterious note as the sun sank below the horizon, casting dark shadows across Whispering Lane. This time, it was a strange phone call rather than a tangible message or enigmatic relic. The other person's voice was weak and garbled, hardly heard over the static. The message was frightening and succinct:

"The chasm remains open. It is waiting below.

The phone conversation ended suddenly, leaving Helen feeling uneasy. The word "abyss" kept repeating in her head, igniting old doubts and anxieties. Could the surface be covered by another layer of darkness? Helen was driven to unravel the enigma and find out what was concealed in the abyss by a feeling of responsibility and curiosity.

Helen started her investigation by looking through historical archives and papers pertaining to Whispering Lane. A fascinating feature she discovered during her study was a set of architectural drawings for the house that showed subterranean rooms and secret passageways. It's possible that the designs were kept secret in the archives because they showed places that were not intended to be viewed.

Underneath the house was a maze of tunnels and chambers, some of which had never been visited, according to the drawings. The portion with the name "The Abyss" caught Helen's eye; it was a big, foreboding room located well below earth. It was said that the chamber had been closed in the past and that no one knew what was inside.

Helen was aware that it would be difficult to enter this secret room. The intricate system of tunnels that led to it, each marked with different symbols and cautions, was shown in the plans. Equipped with this fresh knowledge, Helen prepared herself for a journey into the depths of Whispering Lane.

With the use of contemporary equipment and her understanding from earlier research, Helen set out to investigate the estate's subterranean tunnels. She assembled the necessary equipment, including a strong flashlight, climbing shoes, a radio for communication, and a notepad to record her discoveries.

Entering the subterranean corridors, Helen felt a mixture of excitement and fear. The library's entrance was hidden behind a bookshelf and could only be unlocked by a secret mechanism. The air got cooler and the silence more deafening as she made her way down the steps into the darkness.

The tunnels were small and wet, with old bricks coated in rot and mildew along the walls. Helen's flashlight produced a weird, dim light that twisted and extended the shadows on the walls. The blueprints' marks and symbols corresponded with those on the walls, directing her through the labyrinth of passageways.

Helen eventually arrived at the abyss's entrance after spending hours traversing the tunnels. The door, which was hefty and corroded and had warnings and menacing runes inscribed on it, locked the room. Helen studied the door closely, observing that it seemed to be locked with a complicated mechanism.

Helen was able to force open the door and unlock it with her tools. The room beyond was large and open, with a shadowy ceiling. There was an almost tangible sensation of dread in the musty, heavy air.

Helen was astounded by what she saw as she entered the room. The space was crammed with ceremonial artifacts and odd, occult symbols. An old altar, shrouded in cobwebs and grime, stood in the middle. The altar was surrounded by numerous enormous, elaborately carved figures with frozen looks of despair and agony.

An unearthly force appeared to pulse through the room, and a sensation of malevolence pervaded the air. As Helen got closer to the altar and her flashlight revealed the elaborate carvings and patterns engraved into its surface, a shiver ran down her spine.

Helen's research showed that the room had previously been utilized for sinister ceremonies. It was clear from the symbolism and artifacts that strong and perilous rituals had been held there. Particularly important to these rites was the altar, which may have been used to call upon or channel supernatural energies.

On the altar, she found an ancient diary with fragile, yellowed pages. The notebook belonged to an occultist who had performed ceremonies in the room. The texts described a number of rites, one of which aimed to create a portal to an unidentified world known as "the abyss."

The abyss was depicted in the diary as a region of great power and darkness, home to evil spirits. Although the chamber's rituals were designed to tap into this power, they ended up having unexpected effects. The texts described malevolent entities that had tormented the estate and its occupants, who were released due to a break between worlds.

The room appeared to have a dark aura as Helen read the diary. The stifling mood intensified as the sculptures and symbols seemed to move and transform. The music box's eerie, old tune appeared to reverberate around the room, heightening the tension.

In the room, something solid and unseen seemed to watch her every move. The murmurs from past studies became more insistent, forming a cohesive message:

"It's open; the chasm is black ahead. shut the hole.

It was an obvious message. The terrible energies that had been unleashed were still at work because the ceremonies had created a portal to the abyss. Helen was aware that she had to take immediate action to stop further harm.

Helen concentrated on the journal's directions, determined to seal the gap. The elaborate rituals that were detailed called for certain objects and incantations to be successfully executed. She took the requisites from the room: antique charms, bottles of holy fluid, and ceremonial daggers.

Now that everything was ready, Helen started the ceremony. Her voice reverberated around the room as she chanted the incantations, creating a tense atmosphere. As the altar's symbols began to light softly, the stifling atmosphere appeared to lessen.

As she carried out the ritual, the room became darker, and it seemed as if the shadows were drawing closer to her. The room's intensity increased, turning the whispers into a chorus of distressed voices. The abyss responded to the ceremony; its evil influence was evident.

Helen continued, her resolve unflinching. She was aware that sealing the opening was the only way to stop the darkness from growing. As the ceremony reached its pinnacle, the energy in the room peaked.

The last part of the ceremony was difficult and exhausting. Helen got the impression that she was up against an invisible power as the shadows became ominous and deeper all around her. The murmurs became a deafening boom, and the air crackled with electricity.

Helen finished the ceremony with a last-ditch effort. The oppressive darkness started to fade as the symbols on the altar flared with a brilliant brightness. The atmosphere in the room changed, and the impression of evil dissolved.

The entrance to the shadowy world was shut, and the chasm was sealed. A quiet stillness descended over the room, the voices dying away and the shadows slipping away. There was a sensation of relief and tranquility when the heavy mood subsided.

Tired yet glad, Helen came out of the room. The evil force that had previously haunted Whispering Lane's tunnels and passageways had vanished. Even though the estate still had wounds from its troubled past, it was now peaceful.

Helen thought back on her descent into the chasm. Although the research had unearthed more sinister information, it had also furnished the tools to seal the hole and bring equilibrium back. The evil powers had been subdued, and the ceremony had been effective.

In the days that followed, Helen wrote up her observations in the last chapter of her book, "Silent Screams." The account of the abyss and the rites carried out in the secret room developed into a gripping tale of bravery, tenacity, and the pursuit of truth.

Whispering Lane has changed from being a place of terror and gloom to one of resilience and rebirth. The estate left behind a history of rising above the darkness and discovering light even in the most remote locations. With Whispering Lane's secrets resolved, Helen's quest has come full circle.

Helen carried the knowledge she'd gained from her investigation with her wherever she went. Although the descent into the chasm had been difficult, it had also strengthened her faith in her bravery and tenacity.

She would always carry with her the legacy of Whispering Lane, a constant reminder of the darkness she had encountered and the light she had eventually discovered. A monument to the never-ending search for the truth, the mansion, the cemetery, and the underground rooms all presented a tale of mystery and resolve.

Helen realized she had a lot more work ahead of her. Her trip had only just started, and there were still many mysteries in the world to be solved. She anticipated the future with a feeling of contentment and eagerness, prepared to take on any obstacles that could arise.

The tale of Whispering Lane, with all of its mysteries and darkness, had come to represent Helen's own legacy—one of daring investigation, bravery, and an unwavering pursuit of truth.

Epilogue

After the mystery of Whispering Lane was solved, the village started to reassemble. The once-gloomy estate was now bright with hope, having been purified of its sinister history. In sharp contrast to the foreboding darkness that had before shrouded the home, the sun rose above the horizon, illuminating it and the surrounding area in a warm, golden light.

After serving as the center of Helen Donovan's inquiry, the mansion had undergone significant changes. The stately home was now accessible to the public, with immaculately renovated rooms and freshly painted walls. Regular guided tours told the tale of Whispering Lane's illustrious past and the extraordinary path that brought it back to its former glory. Enticed by the stories of mystery and resolve that had transpired inside its walls, visitors traveled from far and wide.

Helen Donovan, whose name is now associated with the eradication of Whispering Lane's sinister past, has emerged as a local hero. Her work, which was chronicled in her best-selling book "Silent Screams," enthralled readers and earned her recognition as a remarkable writer and investigator. The dangerous voyage through the subterranean corridors underneath the estate, the complex network of secrets, and the eerie experiences were all described in detail in the book.

Helen maintained her composure and attention in spite of the recognition and accomplishment. Motivated by a strong sense of duty and a desire to provide closure to other haunted and mysterious locations, she carried on with her job as an investigator. Her time at Whispering Lane had hardened her resolve, and she brought a mix of empathy, skepticism, and an unyielding determination to finding the truth to every new case.

In addition to physical recovery, Whispering Lane underwent emotional, spiritual, and bodily healing. Though the estate had been purified of its sinister forces, the remnants of its history could still be seen. Once suspicious of the home, the neighborhood has come to accept it as a symbol of resilience and healing.

A committed group of architects, environmentalists, and historians oversaw the estate's renovation. They put a lot of effort into making sure that the home was secure for guests while maintaining its historical character. In order to improve the visiting experience, the restoration work included installing contemporary facilities while carefully maintaining the historic characteristics.

Additionally, the ancient cemetery—once a place of mystery and dread—was renovated. The gardens were well-kept, and the gravestones were cleaned and fixed. The cemetery stood as a memorial to those buried there and a reminder of the difficult past that had been conquered. It was now a calm and reverent area.

Even though Whispering Lane's main riddles had been answered, Helen's labor was far from done. Numerous hints and details that alluded to other unsolved facets of the estate's past had been found by her study. Despite the vast amount of records, artifacts, and firsthand anecdotes she had acquired, there was still a feeling that certain stories had not been conveyed completely.

The mysterious Edward Winslow, whose sinister customs had been crucial to the estate's past, was a topic of considerable intrigue. Winslow's account included inconsistencies and omissions, even in light of the disclosures found in his diary. In order to have a more thorough grasp of Winslow's intentions and actions, Helen was resolved to investigate things further. She looked for more documents and spoke with specialists in occult history.

There were also unanswered issues about the ghosts and otherworldly beings associated with the estate. Even after the ceremonies had sealed off the abyss, there were still sightings and inexplicable events being reported in the area. In order to solve these unanswered questions and provide the impacted people and communities with more closure, Helen intended to carry out more research utilizing her knowledge and skills.

"Silent Screams" has developed into a potent resource for comprehending and dealing with the paranormal, not merely a book. Readers gained an understanding of the nature of terror, the pursuit of truth, and the resiliency of the human spirit thanks to Helen's meticulous details and gripping story.

Along with its influence on historical trauma, the book has spurred a larger discussion on how people and communities deal with and move past their terrible pasts. Many people found resonance in Helen's investigation of Whispering Lane, which combined an engaging narrative with a thought-provoking lesson on the significance of facing and overcoming hidden anxieties.

Others have been motivated to investigate related riddles and look for their own truths by Helen's efforts. Motivated by a renewed interest and resolve, investigators, historians, and enthusiasts assumed the mantle. Beyond the book's pages, "Silent Screams" left a lasting legacy that impacted a new generation of adventurers and storytellers.

Throughout the years, Whispering Lane flourished as a landmark and a symbol of rebirth. The estate developed into a hub for historical and paranormal study, drawing scholarly workers, investigators, and inquisitive tourists from all over the globe. Exhibitions, talks, and movies were just a few of the media that commemorated the house's history and metamorphosis.

Helen's personal legacy was well-established, and her contributions to the fields of paranormal and investigative investigation were well-known. She continued to be a well-known person in her area, giving talks at conferences, writing publications, and coaching young researchers. Her efforts had cleared the path for more research and discoveries, in addition to solving a big enigma.

Helen found personal satisfaction in her relationships and in her constant quest for knowledge. She continued to have strong ties to the neighborhood, often stopping by Whispering Lane to interact with tourists and scholars. Her experiences had shaped her perspective and method of working, leaving a long-lasting effect on her.

Helen was filled with thankfulness and a strong feeling of success as she reflected on her adventure. Her awareness of the supernatural broadened, and her determination was put to the test during the Whispering Lane inquiry, which had been a life-changing event. Her life and career have been molded by the struggles she overcame and the insights she gained.

The trip down Whispering Lane had served as a living example of the strength of bravery, tenacity, and the unwavering pursuit of the truth. The estate had changed from being a place of terror and gloom to one of optimism and rebirth. Future generations will continue to be influenced and inspired by Helen's legacy, which has closed a key chapter in the country's history.

Helen carried the knowledge she'd gained from her investigation with her wherever she went. Her conviction in the significance of facing one's anxieties, pursuing the truth, and accepting the unknown was strengthened by her experiences at Whispering Lane. Although difficult, the voyage was rewarding and left a legacy of bravery, exploration, and discovery.

Whispering Lane was a tale of perseverance, atonement, and the never-ending pursuit of knowledge. The riddles that had long plagued the estate had been solved, and its dark history had been confronted head-on. The legacy of "Silent Screams" would continue to be present in this tale, serving as a constant reminder of both the value of facing the past and storytelling's potency.

Helen realized her trip was far from over as she turned to face the future. She was prepared to take on any obstacles that stood in her way since the world was full of mysteries just waiting to be solved. She welcomed the future with a feeling of contentment and eagerness, driven by the unwavering spirit of discovery and the lessons she had learned from Whispering Lane.

As a monument to the tenacity of truth and the resiliency of the human spirit, Whispering Lane's history and the ghosts of its past would live on. The legend of "Silent Screams" would endure, encouraging people to discover their own truths and face the darkness lurking in the recesses of their own realities.

So the trip continued, led by the fortitude to confront the darkness and the light of enlightenment. With its mysteries and legends, Whispering Lane has endured as a representation of rebirth and hope, a sign that even in the most dire circumstances, there is always a chance for atonement and the prospect of a fresh start.

Don't miss out!

Visit the website below and you can sign up to receive emails whenever Helen Sawyer publishes a new book. There's no charge and no obligation.

https://books2read.com/r/B-A-FZJWB-EZZUD

BOOKS 2 READ

Connecting independent readers to independent writers.

Also by Helen Sawyer

Silent Screams

www.ingramcontent.com/pod-product-compliance
Lightning Source LLC
Chambersburg PA
CBHW051806130726
47987CB00003B/1130